Story A Day May 2013 (31 stories)

by Morgen Bailey

Story A Day May 2013 (31 stories)

by Morgen Bailey

Word Count: © 14,000

Copyright 2013 © Morgen Bailey

'Story A Day May' is the result of an author's challenge to write 31 stories in 31 days in May 2013.

Each story is self-contained and some are connected.

The list of prompts that resulted in these stories can be found at https://morgenbailey.wordpress.com/me/my-writing/short-stories/story-a-day-may/sadm-2013.

Discover other titles (including other 'Story A Day May' collections) by Morgen Bailey at https://morgenbailey.wordpress.com/books-mine.

Thank you for purchasing this book.

If you enjoy it, please encourage your friends to purchase their own copy.

Thank you for your support.

CONTENTS

How The Drabble Came About

Margaret stared at her computer. The cursor flashed encouragingly but both Margaret's brain and the screen were empty.

I need an idea, she thought, but still nothing.

"Write about writing," said a voice from nowhere, so she started…

Margaret stared at her computer. The cursor flashed encouragingly but both Margaret's brain and the screen were empty…

…and soon she'd written a short story, a very short short story, 100 words in fact.

"I know!" she said. "I'll name it after me." So she called it a 'Margaret', but her publisher thought that a terrible idea and renamed it a 'Drabble'.

###

The Quarrymen

You'd come here as a boy, not for years, not realising, remembering, how far down it actually was.

Quarries are high, deep, you think to yourself, and look up at the edge. For a split second you think you see someone, movement, another human looking over the edge, looking at you, but the seagull flies off and leaves the rock, the face-like rock, sitting staring at you, a silent witness to your downfall, the misjudged edge.

You have other company, human, but you know there's no more chance of it helping than the rock-face.

It, him, Charlie – you don't know his second name – was luckier than you, as you fell together, in a fury embrace, you heard his last breath, the expel of air as his body hit the ground, cushioned your fall, the bounce just a foot high.

It's a full moon, a clear night, so you concentrate on the stars, wishing you'd paid more attention in physics. Or was it geography? Closing your eyes, you picture the teacher. Mr Phillpott, double L, double T, the not-so-jolly brown giant. Physics.

You could kick yourself for being so stupid, all the things you could have done, wanted to do, thinking you had forever, but your legs stopped working when you hit dirt.

You start singing 'A Day in the Life' and wonder how yours got so complicated, brought you here.

"4,000 Poles in Blackburn, Lancashire". You wonder how many there are now, then you remember it's 'holes', potholes to be exact, and laugh.

Then you remember; the envelope on the park bench – the bench you use every weekday lunchtime – the envelope stuffed with money, the envelope you'd stuffed into your jacket pocket, for safekeeping until you could go to the police station after work.

Then you remember the hand grabbing your shoulder.

###

It's Not You, It's Me

It's not you, it's me.

No, that's too clichéd.

You're a lovely person but...

Can't do that either.

OK, pull yourself together. Three years isn't that long. She won't go too mad, will she?

Of course she will, what are you thinking?

Oh, God. She'll be here soon. Why didn't I say twelve-thirty? Suppose I should have gone to hers instead of her coming here then I could have done a runner.

There'll be tears of course and I'll never get rid of her. Suppose I could have done it by letter but then she'd have come over anyway... or by text. No, that's the coward's way. I'll come straight out with it. Best to do it quickly. Like a plaster, rip it off in one go and the pain subsides quicker.

Of course she'll say she needs me, can't do without me. Heard it before. You'd think I'd be an expert by now; not being my first. She was the best though. Even I'd admit that. Hard decision but has to be done. Things just aren't working out. I suppose if I hadn't lost my job we could have carried on, but things change, don't they? No point burying your head in the sand. OK. I'll do it then and…

Uh oh, she's here.

Hello. Oh, I love your jacket. Cup of…

Listen, there's something I have to say. Please sit down. Anywhere.

Look, I'm really sorry but there's no other way to put this but I'm going to have to…

I'm going to have to let you go Mrs Jones. I'm sorry but it's economics – I'm going to have to clean my own house from now on.

###

RIP Lenny 'Shades' Froug

Characters as colourful as Lenny 'Shades' Froug don't come along very often and the world is most certainly a darker place without him.

Born Leonard Dennis Froug on the 4th of May 2013, the only son to Dennis Froug Snr and Lillian Froug neé Smith, of Northamptonshire, England, Lenny ignored fashion trends, wearing stripes with spots, snakeskin with floral, and neon with nylon. He earned his nickname not by the sunglasses he wore – he loved direct contact with the sun – but by those worn by the people around him on his particularly colourful days.

As soon as he could talk, Leonard Jnr told his parents that he only had a limited time to live and wanted to fill it with as many experiences as he could. Being an only child, he was not short of love and attention, forming the easy-going personality that endeared him to everyone he met.

As a child, he would venture into his father's shed, help with Dennis Snr's experiments and soon he was trying his own, with success, leading him to ultimately find the cure to the common cold, all strains of cancer known to man, and some unknown, and why the underneath of a yoghurt pot lid always falls the wrong side down (gravital proportion to the square coverage of surface area on each side).

With those achievements, all before the age of twelve, under one's belt – in his case, a skinny Rattlesnake – some would then have taken a step back and settle into a more normal life, but Lenny would regularly be spotted jetting off to war-torn countries where he would take over the peace negotiations and bring them to a satisfactory conclusion – the Gaza Strip now a nature reserve, to parched and famished African countries where he would dance his version of a rain dance, powerful enough to whip up the fiercest of rainstorms, filling the Froug Developments' wells deep enough to last the rest of the century.

One of many figments of English writer, Morgen Bailey's imagination, who herself is famous for killing off many of her characters, she and Leonard had a short (544-word), but endearing relationship, and Ms Bailey is quoted as saying, "I wish I could have known Lenny better. Maybe I'll bring him back to life in a later story."

Those who knew Lenny, are devastated by his early demise and are, at the time of this item going to press, raising funds for his return.

Lenny leaves behind his parents, Dennis and Lillian, and a hamster called 'Pixie'.

The memorial service will be held on 14th May 2013 at the Chapel in the grounds of the Leonard Froug Garden on Mars' Fourth Quadrant, near to the florescent rock pools that Lenny loved so much. A free shuttle bus will be available from all UK airports, where Lenny was a season ticket holder, and Mr and Mrs Froug welcome attendees back to their home, Froug Mansions, which Lenny bought them with the money he received from his seventeenth Nobel Prize.

Those attending are forbidden from wearing black, including underwear – security guards have been instructed to check – and a disco will be held after the service in stretch marquees in the grounds of his home – formerly known as Buckingham Palace – until 'late'.

###

The Thing And The Nameless Page

"What was that?" Willem-Alexander, the ten-minute-crowned King of the Netherlands, scanned the large state room.

His right-hand man, a strange-looking tall, thin Englishman called Nigel Barron-Smythe, followed his employer's gaze. "Sorry your... Highness? I can't see..."

"There! Over there!" the King pointed towards one of the gold and red embossed wallpapered walls.

"May I ask, sir, what I might be looking-"

"There! There! That thing! What is it?"

"Oh yes. I see... I don't rightly know, sir. Perhaps it's a-"

"Spy!"

"Spy, sir? I highly doubt-"

"Someone catch it! Over there before it flies to the... you there! Shut the window!"

A page, whose name no-one knew and whom had almost nodded off during the ceremony which had taken place on the hottest day in the Netherlands' history, leapt to his feet and bolted for the window. He'd not been able to see the 'thing' either but knew he had to do as he told or he'd follow the way of the last page who had missed fulfilling an order and had been turfed out with the recycling. Rumour has it that he'd had to put it out en-route but there had been no witnesses to confirm that, or none that would tell him. After he shut the window, he felt something buzz past his ear. He swung round to see the tiny flapping of wings and an electronic hum.

"Catch it!" he heard as he watched the 'thing' fly towards another open window so he bolted again and managed to get to the window before it reached it. Thwarted again it hovered and spun in circles looking for other exits. Using his initiative, the boy did the same and shut every other window.

The room's gaze loomed on the door, seconds before the thing spotted it.

"The door!" the King shouted and two sentries who had been chatting about which maid-in-waiting they'd get off with at the next door after-ceremony party, slammed the front door which such force that it made the twelve-tier cake, the centrepiece of the festivities, wobble.

Encouraged by his earlier success, the page ran after the 'thing', remembering a bag of treats he had in his pockets for the King's Smoushonds, he retrieved it, threw out the treats – oblivious to the resulting scurrying of claws along the newly-polished floor – and lunged at the 'thing', wrapping it expertly in the bag, twisting the top so it had no chance of escape.

His heart thumped as the object battled to get out. Eventually, the thrashing subsided and the page realised the only sound he could now hear was his heart thumping.

He looked up, around the room, and realised that everyone was staring at him. He swallowed, then as the King beckoned him, the page stepped forward, slowly, head lowered, inching step-by-step.

"Bring it here!" the King boomed and the page quickened along the long old room.

"Run, man!"

The page did as he was told, the bag bumping in his hands, a squeak escaping from it as he did so.

When he reached the King he stopped, held out his hands and bowed his head.

Not sure what to do now, knowing it would likely escape if he undid the bag, the King called on Barron-Smythe.

"I… er, don't know sir. Perhaps if-"

"Anyone else?" the King boomed, looking around the room. His gaze stopped on a short red-faced man standing near to where the King had first spotted the 'thing'.

"You!" the King shouted. "Step forward."

The flushed-faced man looked to his left, right, then pointed to his chest.

"Yes, you! Step forward."

The man did as he was told.

"You look familiar. What's your name?"

"Herbert, sir."

"Herbert… Herbert what?"

"Herbert Wintergrund, sir… your Highness."

"Sir is fine. Who are you?"

"I'm your Science Advisor, sir."

"Oh, so you are. You look shifty, what's the matter with you?"

"I… erm. That…" He looked over at the bag that the page was still holding.

"Yes. Go on! What about it?"

"It's… I'm sorry, sir, but it's mine."

"Yours? Yours? What is it?"

"It's a new type of robot, sir. A present from the Herschel Space Observatory. For you. They thought you might like one – it does all sorts of clever things – and…"

"And?"

"I was going to put it with all your other presents next door but I was late arriving so I stuffed it into my pocket. The little blighter… sorry, your Highness. It escaped and well, went for the light."

The man's face was getting redder and redder, and the page wondered whether he might explode at any moment but then the King burst out laughing.

He clapped his hands twice, whistled for his dogs, and announced that there was enough food next door to feed an army and that they might even play pass the parcel before the disco started.

###

Sally Never Listened

As holidays go, this one was definitely going to be one of the most memorable.

Ted clicked on the right arrow, flicking through the array of photographs. The camera told him he was on number 173 of 1,729. The joy of digital. He was surprised there weren't more, although he had been through them, back in the hotel room, deleting the fuzzy ones. Following wildlife around on safari, there had been plenty of those.

He wished Sally had been there to see the results of the last few but then she would have said that 2D could never replace 3D, having a rhinoceros charge at you, a lion feeding its young, hyenas ripping apart... Ted didn't need to picture that image, he was looking at it.

He looked up as the announcement called for his flight. He picked up his bag and walked to Gate 17. This was the bit he usually loved and Sally usually hated but today he felt the same as she had. They were travelling on different flights and that felt too weird.

The woman in the blue and yellow uniform smiled as she took his boarding pass.

He tried to smile back but knew it was fake.

She read his name and her smile faded. She nodded and held out her arm to indicate his path.

He trudged in line, following the other passengers, some in suits, most in casual clothes. He was still in khaki, a last memory to his two-week vacation, one he didn't want to remember but knew he always would.

As the 'no seatbelt' sign dimmed, and as the man in the next seat asked to be let out, Ted removed his belt then swung his legs round. Ted watched the man walk up the aisle and into the toilet. His wife was staring out the window, hands gripping the seat arms.

Ted laughed, not just to himself, but out loud, to the whole plane and he couldn't stop laughing.

As he started to unnerve the other passengers, an air stewardess approached. "Is everything alright, sir?"

Ted nodded, tears rolling down his face.

"Is there anything I can do, sir?"

Ted shook his head, and wiped his cheek. "I told her…"

"Yes, sir?"

"I told her, my wife Sally, not to get too close but she wouldn't listen. She had to get out the jeep and see for herself. Had to get the best photographs. It was a new camera you see. I bought it for her for our anniversary. She bought the holiday. Very brave, I thought, seeing as she doesn't… didn't like flying."

The stewardess looked at the woman staring out the window.

"Oh, that's not her," Ted said. "No, she's on the next flight."

The stewardess looked puzzled.

"They wouldn't let us travel together. I said I'd wait but-"

"That's terrible," the stewardess said half-heartedly, then went to attend to another passenger.

The woman carried on staring out the window as her husband returned. He took his seat and turned to Ted. "I hope you've not been trying to talk to her. You won't get anything unless you touch her. Deaf as a post. Never listens to a word I say. Still in shock, I suppose."

"Shock?"

"Oh yes, terrifying really. Came a bit too close to a pack of hyenas on one of our jaunts. They said afterwards that a woman did exactly the same thing the day before and wasn't so lucky. I'd told her to be careful but as I said, never listens to a word I say."

###

Quiet And Noisy

The candle flickered while the man crouched over my right ankle. It looked like a candle but I think it was probably a lighter.

Someone had put their briefcase under my head and I could feel the catch digging in. I didn't like to complain because it meant I had a better view of the man. Compared to the pain in my leg, my head was OK. Uncomfortable, not painful really.

Pain's good though isn't it because it means I can feel it, that it's going to be OK. I know there's something on it, my leg, pressing down, so once they get it off they can move me, take me to hospital.

I remember shouting when I first came to, but no one took any notice apart from that one guy and it seemed like I was the only one making any noise, so I stopped. The woman next to me had taken the full force of the metal caving in and I think died instantly because she didn't answer me, and she hadn't stopped talking since she'd got on at Milton Keynes, so I know she would have said something if she could have done.

The lights going out was the worst thing. I hate the dark.

Noise. I had expected there to be more noise but I remember the impact then the quiet. Too quiet. I thought everyone was dead but then I sensed people moving around, shadows, then the pain of my leg took over.

I think the man went to tend to someone else, there are bound to be people worse off than me, but the briefcase is still there.

My head's beginning to hurt a bit now and if I concentrate on that, my ankle isn't so painful. I know I should think of something else, good things, like meeting Josie for lunch.

Oh shit, I must phone her, tell her what's happened, that I'm OK. She'll hear it on the news and worry. She's a worrier when everything's going well, so…

A light! There's a light! Hello? Over here! No, this way…

It's OK. I'll wait. I'm not going anywhere and the train certainly isn't. Not for a while at least. They'll have to clear it out the way, bring in cranes. The poor sods on the later commutes are going to be pretty pissed off. They'll either have to divert... not sure if they can do that.

Buses. They put on extra buses, don't they?

Something doesn't smell very nice. Not like petrol or diesel so that's good. At least we're not going to blow up.

And it's cold. Whatever ran into us... it definitely ran into us because it came into the side, we didn't run into it, must have made a hole... of course it did you stupid sod. Even if it caved the side in there'll be a hole.

Poor train company. I don't usually feel sorry for them... costs me over a grand a year just to get to work and back, but trains are expensive aren't they. I suppose they'll have insurance.

It's still quiet. Can't understand why there aren't people panicking, you know, pulling at things, trying to get out or get other people out. I know someone will come for me... back for me soon. They know I'm alive so they'll come.

Just need to get to my bag. I should have left it on, across my chest like I always do but I wanted to read my book, the latest Kate Atkinson, only just started it so can't even tell you what it's about. It's another Jackson Brodie so it'll be good for sure. Can't help picturing Jason Isaacs now with his lovely blue eyes.

Need to find my bag. Get my mobile then I can ring Josie and she can ring for help. It's fully-charged with plenty of credit. She's my ICE. In Case of Emergency. I was going to ask her to move in with me. Think she'd say "yes". They say something like this tests a relationship. You know, when one person's injured and will need rehabilitation but I'm lucky in that respect too. Josie's a nurse. Senior. Not long had a promotion. That's where we met. At the hospital. I'm a bit accident prone, you see, although this is the worst one yet. Usually just come off my bike... bicycle not motorbike. Not going fast enough to cause any real damage.

It'll get light soon. That'll help. They'll be able to see where everyone is, not rely on torches.

You'd think there would be mobiles ringing. Everyone uses mobiles, don't they? Shout too loudly because of the noise, even quiet electric trains are noisy. That doesn't make sense. Quiet and noisy.

Hello? I'm here! Anyone? Can someone see my bag? I need to ring, Josie. Hello?

###

The Last Thing You Think About

Four hours' sleep isn't enough for anyone but you're used to it. You pretend you're Margaret Thatcher. RIP.

You'd wanted a Jeep ever since you were a boy, since Uncle Frank had given you the white one on the huge wheels and now you were driving one, your pride and joy. Not white, but red – 'Fireman Red', your mother had called it, amongst other names.

Sylvia loves it as much as you do, or that's your impression from her emails, your webcam late nights, your chatroom banter. You could both talk for England, or Scotland in her case.

And now you're going to see her, for the very first time. You'd offered to meet her halfway, drive all the way, but she'd told you how much she'd loved going by train so you'd offered to collect her from the station, in the Jeep. You'd got up early to wash it, in the dark you may have missed a bit. You still smelled the shampoo as you'd started the engine, switched on the radio, too short a journey for a CD.

As you drive, about to cross the bridge just a mile or two away, you imagine her chatting to the person next to her, boring him or her rigid about anything and nothing, probably about you, possibly the Jeep.

You wonder what she'll be wearing, something pretty for sure. She liked to dress up even just for a webcam. Sometimes she'd like to undress too.

You picture her getting on the train at Edinburgh, her floral skirt blowing in the early spring morning breeze, you know it's too early for the sun on her face, too early for warmth. You're with her as she settles into the journey, passing through the beautiful Lake District, the not so beautiful West Midlands then gathering her belongings at Rugby… embarking on the last part of her journey at Milton Keynes.

She's the last thing you think about as you drift off to sleep…

19

What Cost A Human Life?

Jack didn't care that it hurt his shoulder. All he cared about was getting the people out. He'd been to derailments before but this was the first train of the day – he didn't expect there to be many passengers – but on home territory there was a chance he'd be rescuing people he knew.

They'd arrived in the dark, someone heard or witnessed the crash, he didn't know but they'd called 999, and now it was just getting light, making the job easier but not easier. He'd see clearer but then he'd really see what devastation the Jeep had caused.

He knew the driver would be dead. No one would escape a head-on like that; head-on car to side-on train. Only one victor in this entanglement. Not that anyone would call this a victory, with all but two of the eleven or so carriages concertinad in various directions down the embankment, the remaining at right-angles to the track.

Jack blamed the council. The locals had been campaigning for better barriers on that bridge for years but it all came down to money. What cost a human life? he thought as he thumped his right shoulder again at the twisted metal.

A shout went up, "I've found someone!" so Jack stopped pushing, ran over to join his colleague, just as the man behind the caved-in panel stopped breathing.

###

Death and Life

Death

Wonder how long would it take me to reach the ground if I jumped? Ted thinks as he swings his legs in the light breeze. *How many bones would I break? Which part of me would hit the sidewalk first?* He won't of course, would have thought about it a year or so ago but he's turning his life around, working hard, getting off the booze. This is his last bottle of old JD. Mr Daniels and Ted go way back. JD was there when he needed him or thought he needed him but instead of going to the liquor store, he's started going to the café next door. Hadn't even noticed it before, in a world of his own, but it's real cute, a real homely atmosphere with damn fine cups of coffee.

He sits looking at his colleagues, eating their lunch next to him on the girder, chatting away, not a care in the world and thinks, *They're lucky – probably have swell homes, loving wives… gals who make their lunch pails and kiss them off to work. Someone to meet them, hold them, have their supper ready on the table when they get home, someone to care for them… think about them when they're not there.* The 'old' him would have felt all bitter and twisted, but he takes a good hard look at them then at himself, and sees they're no different; just men trying to be happy, getting through life as best they can.

Things on the outside are improving too; the Depression's easing and the mayor's got big plans for the grand city of New York. "Do something about the smog," he says – breathe it in and it chokes you – gonna be a thing of the past. "Look to the future" he says. More high-rise buildings as far as the eye can see, right up to the clear blue water of Rhode Island and out to Martha's Vineyard. So the city is on the up, literally, and that's gonna keep Ted in a job, so he's all for it. Maybe he'll even get out of the Bronx and move to Queens… and one day Manhattan!

So they're constructing the great Empire State Building. Making a new piece of history – John Raskob's vision – he reckons there'll be a million bricks by the time they've finished. Had to be higher than Walt Chrysler's Building. *That Raskob fella must be mad*, Ted thinks, *doing all this just to outdo his rival. Hey, maybe one day I'll even be able to buy one of their cars.*

This girder is boiling – Ted feels like his arse is burning. Fred's got the right idea, bare chest and all.

Ted looks down, at all the people, the worker ants, crawling about their business, never talking to their neighbours. Up here, they're a world away. Ted then spots his apartment block. *Could do with a lick of paint.*

His mind wanders to the girl in the coffee shop yesterday, thinks maybe he'll speak to her tomorrow. "What? Yeah, Joe, it's a fantastic view. Thanks, I'd love a cheese sandwich."

*

Life

The hospital doors fly open and a woman is screaming out "where's my husband? Where's Matthew?"

Twenty blocks away a man kneels down and takes a picture. Little does he know that this innocent snap will be famous worldwide for many years to come. Right now he's thinking about getting the job done before he rushes home to his expectant wife. Their first child is due any day and he can't concentrate. So he continues staring through the viewfinder, hoping for clear shots before getting his equipment together and going home. He looks at the people that compile his picture. Eleven ordinary men but with nerves of steel. He marvels at how they could sit on a tiny, narrow ledge hundreds of feet up in the air. He expects them to look fragile – as if a gust of wind could carry them over at any point – but they're as strong as the girder they sit on. His eye, then lens, focus on a solitary figure at the end. Although he's sitting next to his colleagues, he seems detached – a bit of a loner – and a liquid lunch it would appear. Looks like he has the weight of the world on his shoulders. The photographer wonders what the man is thinking. He puts down his camera and sighs.

The heat of the day hits him. He had thought that it would be cold so high up but it's baking. The white vested guy manages to look cool, clearly used to the heat. Apart from the outsider, the rest of the group seem very relaxed. One lights up a cigarette for a colleague, two others shut their lunchboxes and get to their feet and all but four head back to their site office, casually strolling back along the solid iron tightrope as if they were part of a trained circus. The four remaining men chat for a while, then to the photographer's amazement, swing round to face each other and lay length ways along the girder and go to sleep! He carefully takes more pictures - the shutter sounds deafening as it closes. Today has been one of the best of his life. How many people have the opportunity to see life so raw. Up, natural above the clouds? He feels privileged. Here he is…over a thousand feet off the ground, witnessing the building of the eightieth floor of a planned one hundred and two. As he watches the men nap, he realises that he'll have little sleep from now on but he can't wait.

As his thoughts drift, his wife is going through the early stages of labour.

Senior nurse, Bertha Albright, applies a damp compress to her patient's forehead and holds her hand while a colleague tries, again, to get hold of the father-to-be, willing for the day when people will be able to carry telephones with them. Bertha has assisted in numerous births but the moment a baby arrives still amazes her. She is sure that tonight would be no different.

A visitor in the next ward talks to her friend about a customer in her coffee shop the previous night and hopes that she sees him again before too long.

###

Dating Paradise

The Brington Chronicle's lonely hearts advert read 'gentle giant forties sought for romantic picnics and cinema visits by petite blonde late thirties, reply to Box 147'.

Eve waited for over a week for replies to trickle in but by the second week she'd had fifty.

She sifted through them and found her ideal man, Adam… a match made in heaven!

###

Making Up The Numbers

"Bride or groom?"

Robbie looked at the pews. Plenty of space on the left-hand side. Groom on the left. "Groom."

"Name?"

Robbie went with his usual alias. "Jimmy. Cousin."

The man with the clipboard looked at the left side of his list. It didn't take him long. "Sorry, don't see your name here."

"Ah yes," Robbie started his well-worn speech. "I was a 'no' because I was going to have to work but then at the last minute. You know…"

The man shrugged and added 'Cousin Jimmy' to the list.

Robbie took an end seat halfway down the aisle then turned to the woman beside him, holding out a hand. "Jimmy." He then lowered his voice. "The bride's side really but I thought I'd make up the numbers."

The young lady giggled softly and Robbie noticed her blush.

He'd woken up that grey and gloomy Saturday feeling equally dispirited but now it looked like it might be a good day after all.

###

A Win-Win All Round

Money used to mean everything to Sam. The harder he worked the richer he became… and the quicker it went courtesy of Libby, Mrs Sam Chase. Wardrobes stuffed with carrier bags; Prada, Versace and names he didn't recognise but the lettering gave away their status, the status Libby thought washed off on her.

He'd not told her that he was up for promotion – he knew what she'd want him to do but it meant switching from 'on the road' to behind a desk which in turn meant more time at home, more time with Libby.

George had given him twenty-four hours to think about it. Sam didn't need that long but he knew if he turned it down, George would take longer to ask again but Sam also knew that his colleague Ted was better at his job, a more suitable candidate so it would be a win-win all round if he said "no".

He left work then drove around for a while thinking about what he should do. Libby was at her dance session so he had plenty of time before she was due home.

Having seen the same shops half a dozen times, he found it wasn't helping so went home.

There was a light on in the master bedroom when he pulled into his driveway and assumed Libby had forgotten to switch it off before she went out.

Sam let himself in, put his briefcase down in the hallway, read the post and headed upstairs to change. Opening the door, a predictable sight greeted him; stacks of boxes and bags by the chair, piles of clothes on the floor but unexpected was his wife, dressed in bright red and black underwear. Not only was she not at the gym but she wasn't alone.

Sam took off his jacket and threw it on to the chair. "Hello, Ted."

###

The Ramshackle Writer

On the edge of the mountain, silhouetted against the setting sun, there is a small ramshackle cottage made of wood. It looks like any ordinary cottage but it's the stuff of legends, the owner, the hero of legends.

Or so he thought.

"Tommy!"

No, that's terrible.

On the edge of the mountain, silhouetted against the setting sun, there is a small ramshackle cottage made of wood. Wood collected from the forest at the top of the mountain.

Jack pulled the piece of paper from his typewriter, screwed it up and threw it at the bin. It missed, and became just one of a pile of screwed up pieces of paper.

On the edge of the mountain, silhouetted against the setting sun, there is a small ramshackle cottage made of wood. Inside sits a writer with writer's block.

"How's it coming?" Nancy, Jack's long-suffering wife looked over his shoulder. "Oh dear."

"Yes, exactly."

"It's a bit 'Dark and stormy night'."

"I know, but it's the prompt for today."

"Can't you change it?"

"We can but I like to stick with what we're given."

"It is only for fun."

"And to put on my blog. By five o'clock."

Nancy looked at her watch. Five twenty-five.

"I know. I can backtime it."

"Backtime? Is that even a word?"

"Don't know. Backdate is."

"If you used a computer like everyone else, it would underline it if it wasn't a word."

"It doesn't matter. I'm a writer, I can make up words."

"Why don't you?"

"Why don't I what?"

"Use a computer like everyone else."

"It feels… I don't know. It feels more authentic. Like Stephen King. Very… Secret Window."

"Terrible movie."

"I know. It's all a dream and all that. But I'm more productive this way. My ideas flow better."

"They're not flowing today."

"I know, but that's not the typewriter, it's the prompt."

"Then pick another one."

"No, I'll persevere."

Nancy shrugged. "OK, but don't blame me if…" The rest was lost as she went into the kitchen.

"Another prompt," Jack mumbled as he pulled out the paper, screwed it up and launched it at the bin. It hit the edge but fell in. He clapped, laughed and put another piece of paper into the typewriter, twisting down the end, until the paper was sticking out a couple of inches from the top.

"Another prompt…"

He sat up straight, hovered his fingers, claw-like, over the keys and started tapping.

It was a dark and stormy night…

###

Beyond The Blue Horizon

Tel stared out through the treble-layer glass at the blue horizon. It seemed to be growing a shade darker every day but he looked down at the printer, at the reports, and they didn't show anything out of the ordinary; the heartbeat lines pulsating in rhythm with no hint of a deviation. If there was an attack due then the machine wasn't sensing it.

There was only one other explanation that Tel knew, or rather had heard of. It had never happened in his lifetime.

It was going to rain.

He couldn't say anything. They'd laugh at him.

No one knew what effect real water would have on man-made water. Would they just blend or would one substance react with the other? Kill the other?

Maybe this was the attack after all. They, the powers that be, had said it was to be an air attack. Could it be something as simple as rain?

"Rain?" an alarmed voice said behind him.

Tel swung round. "Stop doing that!"

"What?" Farbe looked innocent.

"Sneak up on me… read my mind."

I only read the good bits, Farbe said not moving his mouth. "Now what's this about rain? You know we haven't had that since-"

"And we won't," Tel interrupted. "The reports are fine, everything's fine." He gave a nervous chuckle.

"Then why is the sky getting darker, bluer?"

Tel turned to look at it. "You've noticed it too?"

"No." Farbe leaned in. "I was listening to you."

Tel stepped backwards, standing, not by accident, on Farbe's foot.

"Ow!"

Tel faced his colleague. "How long have you been standing there?"

"Since just after you were thinking about what you'd like to do to Evetha." Farbe grinned.

"Before…? Before! How?"

"I'm a Mark IV, remember." He tapped the side of his white metal-clad head. "Improved sensors." He then shook his foot to clear the pain, which appeared to do the trick. "Right," he said, as if taking authority. "What are we going to do about this rain?"

Tel shrugged.

"There's a contingency plan somewhere isn't there?"

Tel's eyes lit up. He opened a drawer under one of the desks and pulled out a red file.

Farbe stepped forward to join him.

Turning to the index, Tel ran his finger down the alphabetical list then read out, "Railway incidents… Raised blood pressure… Raisins stuck in throat." He looked over at Farbe. "Raisins? They've got raisins but nothing about rain? What are we supposed to do?"

"Maybe you're wrong."

"I don't think so. I can feel it in my…"

"Water?" Farbe laughed.

"Bones. I've just got this horrible feeling…"

"Then you should tell someone."

"They won't believe me."

"I believe you."

"No, you don't."

Farbe put on his sincere expression. "I do."

"Then you tell them."

"Oh, I can't do that. I'm only a Mark IV."

"What were you saying about improved…?"

"Sensors. But we're still young. No Mark IV I know of has got past Assistant, and I'm not even there yet." He hesitated then thrust a finger in the air. "I know!"

"Yes?"

"Let's ask a Mark V!"

"What? There are no Mark Vs."

"Yes there are. There's one. It was in the paper." Farbe held up his right hand, palm facing Tel, and a screen within it burst into life.

Tel read the first few lines then looked back at Farbe.

"That's no good. We don't know where it is."

Farbe sighed. "If you'd read a bit further you'd have got to the bit saying where it was going to be delivered."

Tel looked out the window, to the right of the horizon, to the city complex and the thousands of home-pods. "Go on, where."

"Here."

Tel turned to Farbe. "Here? Really? When?"

Before Farbe could reply, an electronic swish sounded behind them and a door slid open. It was the same sound as they used on the first Star Trek TV series, Tel's boss a big fan, had been insistent on it.

They stood there open-mouthed as a gold version of Farbe glided in. "Hello, I'm New."

"We know," Farbe said first.

"No, my name is New."

"Oh," Tel said. "And erm… what do you do?"

"Everything," New replied, his voice changing tone with every word, like a gentle stream on a summer's day.

"Everything?" Tel repeated.

"He does," Farbe said, looking at Tel, then scrolling down the text on his palm screen. "He even tells the future." Farbe turned back to face New. "We have a question for you."

"I know," New said.

"Of course," Farbe laughed. "You can tell the future."

"Rain," Tel butted in.

New faced Tel and gulped.

###

Progress

"Remember when this was fields?"

"I do. Not all that long ago."

"Ten years, just over. A month or two after Sally and Ben got engaged. They were one of the first to buy here."

"Oh, yes. Paid a fortune too, if I remember."

"A small fortune, yes, but they wanted eco-friendly and the King was pushing for that so of course everything cost more."

"King Charles? Was he on the throne already by then?"

"Not long before. 12th June 2014. Ben's thirtieth birthday. The Queen abdicated on Sally's; 15th May. Guess it came as a bit of a shock so it took them a while to sort out the paperwork."

"Sally and Ben?"

"No. The coronation. The government."

"Oh, yes. Nice party. This drinks party, I mean, not the government…"

"Isn't it? Not many faces I recognise though."

"Me neither. Bit of a relief to see you, if I'm honest."

"Likewise. They've started digging up old Jack Tyler's land."

"Have they? For houses?"

"A thousand."

"No!"

"Yeah. Can you imagine?"

"Not really. A thousand on the bit of land behind the farm?"

"Oh no, the whole thing."

"What? What's going to happen to the house?"

"Flatten. I think they've done it already."

"That lovely old-"

"Progress."

"So where's Jack gone?"

"You haven't heard?"

"Heard what?"

"Heart attack."

"No! When?"

"When he got the letter offering seventy million."

"Seventy million? What happened to that?"

"The son got it."

"Jack had a son?"

"Lives in the States. Married a girl over there and stayed. Didn't want the farm, of course."

"Who would when offered that much?"

"The son."

"Never saw him visit."

"Think they fell out."

"Reconciled after this death, though, didn't they? A thousand homes. Wow. The council will grant anything these days."

"It's the government push… since the shuttles started bringing the… you know, the legal aliens."

"Of course, but people are leaving too, though, aren't they?"

"Not as many. We have more resources here."

"True, but Mars is young and you'd think exciting."

"Fine for single people, but most have families these days, especially given the couple's bonuses shooting up since the housing crisis came to the fore, and most wives would be more traditional, you know, happier to stay put. They'll wait for Mars to be established then they'll go. If they go. Most can't afford it."

"Can if they have farms to sell."

"Yeah. If only…"

"Better mingle."

"Me too. Nice to see you again."

"You too."

###

Worth Every Penny

You look at the advert in your hand then at the car. The words 'Trades', 'Description' and 'Act' spring to mind.

"And the top speed is…?" you ask the old man who's staring at his car lovingly.

"Had her over a hundred-and-thirty a few times." The old man steps closer. "When no one was looking of course."

You look back at the paper, and the price. "Two thousand is a bit steep."

"Worth every penny," the man says, stepping back and tilting his chin. "Spent almost that much doing her up."

You look at the car, its red rusting bodywork and wonder where the money could have gone.

The old man looks at you and nods. He shuffles towards the bonnet and lifts it up.

The sun hitting the engine almost blinds you and you pull down the sunglasses that had been perched on the top of your head. "Wow," is all you can say.

###

Bubble And Squeak

It was the bubbles in the champagne that got Poppy tipsy after just one glass.

"You're getting no sympathy from me," Mark said, slamming the car door making Poppy whine. "Seatbelt," he ordered, a little too loudly.

He started the engine as Poppy grabbed the belt and brought it in front of her stomach. She was about to click it in place when Mark thrust his foot on the accelerator making the car lurch then cut out.

Poppy put a hand up to her mouth and closed her eyes. "Please, Mark," she said as he restarted the car.

She opened her eyes again as they drove away from the hotel and headed for the motorway. Pulling at her purple and pink bridesmaid's dress, she debated what to say to break the silence. "Please don't be angry with me, Mark."

"I'm not angry with you, Poppy," he replied. "I'm angry with myself. I always knew it was you I should have been marrying. Your sister will never forgive us."

###

Wreckage

Jamie stood in the wreckage of his ransacked house, trying to take it all in.

He didn't even know where to start. Was there a start?

He had to call the police, he knew that, but on this side of the city it was a fairly regular occurrence so he also knew the chances of catching anyone, of them being stupid enough to leave any fingerprints, was slim, but he had to for insurance purposes.

Insurance. "Shit!" Wasn't it due around now?

He went to the kitchen, put on a pair of yellow Marigold washing up gloves then bolted up the stairs to the back bedroom.

He looked at the bookcase but it was empty, the files scattered over the floor. He searched through them, the fact they were all the same shade of blue adding to his frustration.

When he found the right one, he clasped it to his chest, went to the landing phone and dialled 999.

He then returned downstairs, filled the kettle and opened the folder. The reminder letter from Wickett & Pringle lay on the top. Jamie scanned the text then found the renewal date; 17th July. It was the 19th.

Jamie slumped in the chair and hung his head over the paperwork. He stuck out his tongue and blew a half-hearted raspberry.

He hadn't expected a rapid response to his phone call but had only just made himself a cup of tea, surprisingly difficult to do while wearing washing up gloves, when he saw the flashing blue light outside.

He opened the front door as two officers approached it. He then spotted the ambulance.

"Are you the owner?" the taller of the two asked. Jamie read the officer's name badge. Townshend.

38

Jamie nodded. "I only called the police. I didn't ask for an ambulance."

"Step inside, please, sir," Townshend ordered.

Jamie took a step back.

"All the way, please," his colleague, Rylett, added.

Jamie reached the lounge doorway, still facing the officers. "I don't understand. What's going on?"

"Where's the woman?" Townshend asked, dropping the 'sir'.

"What wo-?"

"Never mind. Rylett, you look upstairs. I'll stay down here with Mr…"

"Dawson. Jamie Dawson. But…" He watched Rylett go upstairs then Townshend ushered Jamie into the lounge.

Townshend tilted his chin towards the mess that was surrounding them. "So, Mr Dawson. Domestic or were you looking for something?"

"No. Neither. I've been out, only just got in. I don't know… what woman? Who-?"

But before he could continue, Rylett appeared. "She's up there. We're too late."

"What?" Jamie asked as Townshend strapped handcuffs to his gloved hands.

###

Before Jessica

Jessica drew her tongue across her upper teeth. The drink was supposed to console her but the shop assistant had put in too much ice.

She took another sip and grimaced. Chocolate. She needed chocolate, the epitome of comfort food.

Epitome. Not a word most sixteen-year-olds knew the meaning of, but the dictionary was one of her favourite books.

Simon, her older-by-two-years brother, would laugh at her, her head always buried in something; fiction, non-fiction, Jessica didn't mind which. She especially loved the law so read crime novels, not the gory type where there's blood oozing on every other page, but clever crime, cosy; Agatha Christie and the likes.

Simon was more of a science-fiction, Doctor Who fan, although he'd not be seen dead with a book in his hands, the TV far more realistic in his opinion, video box sets his only request at Christmas and birthdays.

Jessica didn't see the point of half-watching a programme, face peering from behind a cushion. She'd rather sit glued to every second, every frame, appreciating the work the cameramen had put in. It was an art. Everyone involved were artists.

She'd loved to do something in films, not act, she had a terrible memory, but something behind the scenes. In case it didn't work out, she'd enrolled on a typing course, second week in.

She looked at her at chewed nails. Long nails were impractical on a typewriter, even electronic ones. A good excuse, she thought as she slurped the remnants of her orange juice.

###

Leaving A Gap

~~Hello diary.~~ Hello Diary. Mum bought you for me for Christmas and I'm so excited. I ~~doh~~ ~~doent~~ don't know whether to wait until January the first or start now. Next year is a whole week away and we've had such a great Christmas Day so I think I'm going to start now. I am. OK, new line.

Dad was being a bit quiet today. I think he ate too much. So did I.

Mum was busy cooking so hers was colder than ours because she wanted to do the washing up before she had hers and she had less than us, I don't think she was hungry. She told us not to wait so we didn't. I felt a bit bad but Dad said we should do as we were told so we did. I didn't eat as quickly as him because I wanted to still be eating when Mum came to the table. Oh yes, you won't know that the kitchen table is now in the dining room. Yes, we have a dining room! So the kitchen table is now the dining room table. I don't think it minds. In fact I think it's really happy. I'm happy too because I like it here. It's bigger than our old flat. This one has an upstairs, where we sleep, which means I have to come downstairs if I need a drink of water when I can't sleep. Mum suggested – suggested means that she was giving me a good idea – but I didn't think it was a good idea so I did not do it. She suggested that I take a glass of water to bed, when I go to bed, but it'll get warm. I said that to her and she said it was OK. This place is warmer than the flat. It has fancy white windows with two pieces of glass in each one! So I didn't bring any water to bed. I don't mind getting up and going to the kitchen because I get cold and my bed is still warm when I get back.

I'm going to say goodnight now because I'm tired and it's late. Nearly ten oclock. If I get up to get some water, I might say hello but nothing will have happened for me to report other than me going downstairs and getting the water so I probably won't.

~~Good morning diary. It is December the 26th.~~

December 26 – Boxing Day

Good morning Diary. I forgot that diaries have the dates at the top so I've gone back to yesterdays and put December 25 – Christmas Day at the top, just in little writing because I didn't leave much space.

This is not a normal diary because it doesn't have the dates at the top. Mum said she didn't want to buy me one of those because it would mean that I could only write on one page and she said I should write whatever I wanted. She called it a journal – she helped me spell it – but it sounds silly to say Hello Journal so I have called it you a Diary. Not a diary with a little d because you are a person like me because when I read you, you talk to me.

There are lines so I can write straight. I like it. I try to make my handwriting nice, like I was ~~teached~~ tort at school. That was a long time ago. I'm too old to go to school now.

Nothing really happens at home so I don't know if I would fill a whole page anyway but it does mean that I can put two days on one page if I want to. I left a gap on yesterdays because we had a busy day so I can tell you what happened. I will do it later. I will not forget. I have a good memory.

Mum is calling me to go downstairs for breakfast so I am going now but I will write more later.

I have put a line there because it means that I am not here for a while.

December 28 – The Day After The Day After Boxing Day

Sorry I have not written anything for two days. I have left lots of lines so I can write what happened yesterday. I have put in the title. December 27 – The Day After Boxing Day but I don't want to write it yet.

I think you will want to know what happened so I will put a little ~~now~~ here.

Mum has left us. I think that's why Dad was quiet but he has not said much. He said she packed a few things in a bag and left in the middle of the night. I wanted to go into their bedroom to see which things she took. She showed me her clothes so I know which ones are missing but Dad will not let me. I asked him when she left, what time, but he ~~shaked~~ shook his head.

I said before, to you, that I usually wake up and get a glass of water but I didn't. I would have seen her leave, tried to stop her. I would have woken up if she left ~~would not I~~?

I think it's going to be OK. Just with Dad and I. Mum did the cooking ~~and shopping~~ and cleaning but I can do that. I can do the cooking. I watched Mum. I can clean too. I know what to do.

Dad will do the shopping. Sometimes he goes to the pub for a drink. ~~He is not a alko~~ He does not drink much. He asked me if I wanted to go with him but I don't like to go out.

I have to go. Dad wants me. He needs me. So I am leaving a gap.

###

Human Unfriendly

Natalie looked under the sofa, Patch's usual hiding place, but other than dust and a couple of his toys, it was empty.

She was less bothered about the gun lying on the coffee table. She'd not seen it before, it was the longest he'd ever had, but Granddad was often lying strange objects around the house; this one likely to be a new addition to his collection.

One thing he never did though was take Patch for a walk. Letting him out in the garden was as good as it got, and she hoped that was what he'd done but Granddad was not what you would call animal-friendly, or human-friendly. He barely tolerated Natalie.

Natalie's attention then turned to the running water in the kitchen. Washing hands or washing up? It had been running for too long to be either.

She walked through to the kitchen, expecting to see some sign of life but the only thing moving was the water, so she turned if off and tried the back door. As she thought, it was locked.

Looking around the room there was nothing out of place. Granddad, if nothing else, was fastidiously clean and tidy. She returned to the lounge and called again, waiting for paws or footsteps but the house gave nothing away.

Upstairs was no different; everything in its place. Coming down the stairs, she looked at the coat hooks and Patch's lead was still there so a miracle hadn't happened.

She called for them again but knew it was futile.

The gun was the only thing that had changed since she'd left that morning so she went to it, knelt down, and touched it, using the backs of her fingers, she knew better than to leave fingerprints. The gun was warm.

###

It Wasn't Me

Gwen looked down at the ripped toy, then into the big brown eyes staring up at her.

"It wasn't me."

"Really? Then who was it? There's only you and I here."

The big brown eyes kept staring. "Alright. I confess. It was me but it's your fault for-"

"Henry! You've become so cheeky since we gave you the ability to talk."

Henry wagged his tail.

Gwen was pretty sure that had enhanced since they, her and her boss, Dr Temple Horne, had injected the dog with the experimental speech drugs. "I thought that toy was your favourite."

"I was only playing."

"It's got dribble all over it. You were shaking it weren't you?"

Henry nodded. "It's what we do. We're dogs. We chase rabbits, cats and things."

"Anything that moves, I know."

"So you give me a cat toy and I'm going to-"

"Chase, Henry. You didn't need to rip it to shreds."

"It's not shreds. An ear's come off, that's all."

"What did I say about you being cheeky?"

"Just speaking my mind."

"If I'd known..."

"What?"

"Nothing. Never mind. Now, Dr Horne and I have some things we want you to do. When we ask you questions, we want your honest answers, OK?"

Henry nodded.

Right on cue, Dr Horne, entered the lab, studying a clipboard. "How is he today?"

"I'm well, thank you."

Dr Horne looked up from his notes. "Henry?"

Henry smiled. "That's me."

"So everything's OK. Voice alright?"

"More than alright," Gwen answered. "Can't shut him up."

"I did think it was weird to start with," Henry said. "I could hear myself. Of course I could always hear myself but it's like it was clearer, louder and…"

Dr Horne watched Henry's lips move as he waffled on. "Your lips are moving."

Henry stopped mid-stream. "Of course. I'm no ventriloquist."

Dr Horne laughed, looked at Gwen's scowl and laughed again.

Henry turned to Gwen. "You said you had some questions?"

"Yes. Dr Horne?"

The doctor looked back down at his clipboard. "Number one. How do you feel?"

Henry frowned and repeated, "I'm well, thank you."

"Number two. Has anything else improved since the implementation of the medication?"

"'implementation of the medication'," Henry mimicked. "Like what?"

"Memory? Vocabulary? Desires? Motivations?"

"Erm…"

"Maybe a bit too much all at once," Gwen suggested.

"No, it's OK," Henry said. "Memory. The same, I think. Born, eat, poop, chew…" He looked at the toy. "I couldn't help it."

"That's OK, Henry," Dr Horne soothed. "That's what they're there for. Any frustrations?"

"Apart from it not being a real cat?"

Dr Horne laughed and put a large tick in the 'sense of humour' box.

"You asked about vocabulary," Henry continued.

"Yes," Gwen butted in. "And Desires, Motivation."

"Vocabulary. Now I like hearing the sound of my voice-"

"We can tell," Gwen mumbled, receiving a dirty look from Henry.

"It's not like I've studied a dictionary since you gave me that stuff."

"Interesting," Dr Horne said while chewing on the end of his pen.

Henry didn't find that interesting at all. He'd quite like to spend his time studying not only a dictionary but an encyclopaedia as well, but thought that a step too far at this early stage. "As for desires. I still desire to rip up…" He looked up at Gwen and paused. "Desire to play with my toys. That was an accident. Motivation, being given a fake cat is a good one."

"Very good." The doctor nodded and jotted more notes. "Question four. If you could be any animal what would you be?"

Henry tilted his head.

"Would you like me to repeat that?"

Henry straightened his head again. "You mean you can change me into something else?"

Dr Horne laughed. "Of course not, Henry. We can only work with what we have."

"That's a silly question then isn't it?"

"It's hypothetical."

Henry now wished he'd had that dictionary.

"Pretend," Gwen added, seeing the expression on his face.

"A giraffe."

The two white-jacketed humans looked at each other.

"A giraffe?" Gwen asked.

"Why a giraffe, Henry?"

"It's obvious, isn't it?"

The doctor shook his head.

"Because all I see all day are ankles. Knees if I'm begging, which I don't plan on doing again any time soon, by the way. If I was... were a giraffe I'd be able to see anything, wouldn't I? Even more than you. Any more questions?"

Dr Horne nodded. "A few but I think that's enough for today."

Gwen looked at him startled, so he beckoned for her to join him in the corridor.

Henry watched them leave then turned his attention to the one-eared cat. "They'll be giving that stuff to you next, although they'd have to sew your ear back on or you wouldn't be able to hear their questions properly."

He then looked back at the glass pane in the door, saw the ecstatic expression on Gwen and the doctor's faces. "If you're like that now, just wait until I show you what I can **really** do."

###

Scratch, Squeak, Bark

Natalie's attention turned away from the gun and to a scratching noise above her head.

As she walked up the stairs, the sound reminded her of the Glis-glis her father had found in the ceiling of their old garage.

The scratching stopped as she reached the landing and turned to face the front bedroom. She edged forward and paused in the doorway.

"Hello!" she whispered, then lunged at the wardrobe as the scratching resumed, and pulled open the door. There looking up at her with weary eyes was Patch, her eight-year-old Jack Russell. His tail wagged slowly but then realised who he was looking at and began squeaking. The squeaking turned to a bark as he looked beside her.

She stood up but before she could turn round, a heavy object struck her head and she dropped to the floor.

###

All-Inclusive Package

I flinched as the cell door slammed. You'd think it would be worst the first night but then I still had hope.

It'll be a month on Friday and they're still wrangling, 'them' being the British Embassy and Thai authorities.

There's no doubt about Simon, but we're being tried together and I'm a grey area.

Carrier. Mule. Whatever you want to call me. 'Wife' is what Simon calls… called me. Wife of thirty-seven days. The dream holiday, all-inclusive package; wedding, honeymoon – romantic ceremony for four… five if you include the celebrant, our hotel manager. They're multi-talented over here. Too, as it turns out is Simon; liar, con artist, thief. Not sure if he's a cheat yet but it doesn't matter anymore. We'll see each other in court and that'll be that.

The lawyer they've given me says I could get ten years. Ten years! For carrying my suitcases, but not checking them properly.

Did I pack them myself? Of course you're going to say, "yes", even if you didn't, which I did. Thought I had. Had.

Did I, at any time, leave them unattended? You're going to say, "no". Of course I hadn't left them alone, not since we'd left the hotel. The taxi driver loaded everything into his boot and I sat beside him all the way, nearly an hour. I get travel-sick so Simon let me sit in the front. He's… he was good like that. We didn't stop once so no way anyone could have interfered with them.

Then we went straight from the taxi to check-in. That went OK, as did the X-Ray but I knew it would because we had nothing new in our hand luggage, all our souvenirs were in our cases. The security check was OK. They lingered over Simon's passport but let us through. You always feel guilty even when there's no need. We were fine on the trip out so there was no reason not to be on the return.

My lawyer's due back today. Don't know when but…

50

It's just how you imagine it to be here, how you might have seen it on TV. I'm lucky. I have a corner to myself, and a seat. Some have to stand. We all have our spaces, like a book club meeting. Someone goes and you get to take their place, try to get a place before it's offered to you and they don't let you forget it. We've just hit fifty in here. I count every time I wake up but it only ever changes in the day. No one comes at night. The women are mostly around my age, mid to late thirties. We only get one shower a day and clean clothes once a week so it's not nice but we're all in the same... boat.

At least we had our holiday. Could have been caught arriving but then as far as I know Simon bought the stuff here, or was given it. I don't know. They interviewed... interrogated us in separate rooms, told me all about him, who he really is. His name's the same, before you think that he's that kind of con man, but all the other things he's done... I'm just one of a long line, at the end of it, I guess, but when you're in love...

Hello? Yes. Yes, that's me.

###

His Job Depended On It

The corpulent official stared down at the cream-filled doughnut. He smiled and sighed, patting his generous stomach. He knew this delicious treat was doing him no good but he had to do it. His job depended on it.

He turned round in a panic as he heard a scratching noise behind him, but then remembered it was his son's turn to look after his class' hamster.

Turning back to the plate, he picked up the doughnut and settled into reading the paper's front page article: 'Twin Town's New Totem Pole', being careful not to spill anything down his Santa suit.

###

Eight A Year

"Another bank holiday!"

"We only get eight a year."

"Eight! That's one every... six weeks. Plus all your other holidays."

"Six and a half, but we deserve them."

"And I have to pay for them."

"Twenty days a year isn't as much as some companies."

"Be grateful you get any. They don't in the States, you know."

"I'm pretty sure they get Thanksgiving."

"Yes, alright. And Christmas, but they certainly don't get twenty days... So, what are you going to do with yours?"

"Heading to Brighton for the day."

"Nice. The weather is supposed to be good."

"And you?"

"Barbeque."

"That'll be fun. But it'll mean it'll rain. Beach, barbeque, Bank Holiday, rain."

"Let's hope not. Right, I'll let you get on. See you on Tuesday."

"Yes. See you then. Oh..."

"Yes, Tom?"

"Can you tell Mum 'thanks' for the jam. It's lovely."

"Will do."

###

Billy No Mates

They say we all have good and evil within us, meet Tom and Billy.

Billy looked up. "What are you doing here?"

"Come to see you."

"Why?"

"Because..." Tom sat down. "Because I'm your brother."

Billy leaned forward. "No, Tom. You're a horrible little oik."

"Billy!"

"You're a ... little ..."

"Don't!"

"You snitched on me. What do you expect?"

"I'm sorry. I said I'm sorry."

"Too late now."

Tom looked around the room. He was surprised to see just two others, talking, ignoring them.

"You're not so snow white yourself."

"What?"

"Mr Taylor's front garden."

"I've never been in Mr Taylor's front garden."

"Picky little shit! You weren't in his garden."

"You said-"

"Not IN his front garden. I saw you drop litter into it."

"Didn't."

"Did."

"I didn't!"

"Did too!" Billy spoke loudly enough for the others to turn to him.

54

Tom noticed the scared look on one of their faces. "When?"

"The day before I… the day before."

"I… oh."

"Yes! See? Not the darling son Mum thinks you are, are you?"

"It wasn't litter."

"Rubbish."

"It wasn't! It was a snail!"

"What?"

"A snail. I almost treaded on it."

"Trod."

"I almost trod on it, then, and I didn't want anyone else to squish it so I picked it up. Mr Taylor has a lovely green garden so I dropped it over his fence."

"Mmm…"

"Is that why-?"

"They're going to keep me in here for years."

Tom looked down into his lap. "I know."

"And you knew you'd get me into trouble when you snitched."

"I had to."

"No… you… didn't."

"I liked Mr Taylor!"

"You didn't know him."

"He said 'hello' when I walked past and he was outside. He was nice to me."

"He wasn't nice to me."

###

Talking When We Could Be Walking

"Oh no! Is it really eleven already?"

"You've got plenty of time."

"Dad, I'm supposed to be there at midday."

"And only it's a ten-minute drive. Fifty minutes easily."

"I don't want to be there on the dot! I want to be a bit early."

"Brides aren't supposed to be early. It's tradition."

"I certainly don't want to be late. What time is the car booked for?"

"Eleven. You know that. It's downstairs, but we have it until it drops you and Alex at the reception."

"Have you spoken to Alex today?"

"No, Suzie. Why would I?"

"Just to check that everything's OK."

"It'll be fine. Stop panicking."

"Something's going to go wrong. I can feel it."

"Nothing's going to go wrong. You're a secretary. Everything's precision-timed."

"But I should have been ready by now."

"You look ready to me and you look gorgeous. Your mother would have-"

"Dad, don't! You'll set me off and Tracey's done my make up."

"Is there anything else to do?"

"Erm… no, I don't think so."

"OK. So you're ready. The bridesmaids are ready."

"The bridesmaids! How are they getting there?"

"Uncle Nick's taking them. Don't panic!"

"Oh, yes. Sorry. I know. I'm making-"

"A mountain out of a proverbial molehill. It's your prerogative but just enjoy the day."

"OK. Thanks, Dad."

*

"What was that noise?"

"Just a bad gear change, I think. Nothing to worry about. The driver knows what he's doing."

"I knew we should have left earlier."

"But then we'd be too early and we'd be driving round in circles."

"You're right as alw- What was that?"

"It didn't sound good."

"We're slowing down! There's smoke!"

"Oh dear. Never mind, we'll get a lift with Uncle Terry and the bridesmaids."

"Everyone else has left already."

"So he'll be available to come and get you. Ring him on your mobile."

"I don't have my mobile, Dad. Wedding dresses don't come with pockets."

"But you've got a bag."

"Horseshoe, flowers. Two hands so no, no bag. I told you you should get a phone."

"Never needed one. You only live round the corner."

"Oh, Dad. What are we going to do?"

"Maybe the driver's… no? That's ridic- You'd think he'd have some way of communicating with his company. How is he supposed to tell them… We'll have to walk. We've got time."

"It's at least a mile."

"We've got half an hour. Twenty minutes a mile."

"Maybe we can find a phone box."

"Have you got change?"

"No. I told you, no pockets. Don't tell me you don't have any."

"I've only brought my wallet. It doesn't have a change"

"So you've got money."

"While we're sitting here talking when we could be walking."

"I'm going to cry."

"Don't. Tracey's done your make up. Come on. If we chat while we're walking we'll be there in no time."

"Thanks, Dad."

"That's what I'm here for. It's alright, Frank. Not your fault. We'll make our own way but please be there when we come out. OK? Thanks."

"Oh, God."

"What?"

"I didn't think about getting to the reception."

"Don't worry, Suzie. We can take Uncle Terry's car. There'll be plenty of other people who can take the bridesmaids."

"This is not how I had it planned."

"I know but as long as you get there."

"These shoes are killing me already. I only needed to walk-"

"What?"

"The police car's stopping. You don't think…"

"You never know."

"He's getting out, opening the back door. Yes, Dad!"

"Hello, Officer. St Barnaby. The car broke… It's very kind of you."

"Yes. Thank you!"

*

58

"Thank you again, Officer."

"Thank you so much."

"Hurry, Dad!"

"It's five to. We're fine. Slow down. Breathe."

"Yes, Dad. OK. Calm, Suzie… calm."

"Step… step… three… four… There's the music. We're here. We've arrived. You're going to get married."

"Look! There's Alex. Doesn't she look lovely?"

"Yes, Suzie. Suit and all, but yes, she looks lovely."

###

Petrified

The second time I met Paul Trollope, I was a completely different person. He'd obviously exhausted his luck up north so was trying his hand at the Home Counties, my Home Territory. Unfamiliar to him so for once I had the upper hand. And I made the most of it.

Having Tyler with me helped. It kept me level headed although he didn't take to him. Tyler to Paul. Dogs aren't stupid. I did meet a stupid greyhound once, dull as a ten-watt bulb, but Tyler's a full hundred-watt. Low energy but full power when it's needed. And I found Paul's weakness. Dogs. Had always been scared of them. Petrified in fact and although Tyler is not much more than ankle height, he packs a mean punch, a hearty bite when given the right word. Trollope. Not just a coincidence. As I said, he's a clever dog.

Turns out Paul's car had broken down on the way to meet a woman in one of the villages just this side of Aylesbury and he'd got lost – followed the Sat Nav. I've been there before; not doing a U-turn in Uxbridge, but that's another story.

So there he was walking along the country lane in the middle of nowhere, the (stolen) VW flashing its little heart out a few yards down the road and what does he come across but a converted windmill. My windmill. It's the only building around and there's a light on, so he clicks the gate and walks up the needs-some-attention driveway before knocking on the door. Tyler barks and whilst he normally barks at anything that catches his attention, it's not often that it's followed by him running to the front door. We don't get many visitors – most people don't bother. It's either too far or they take one look at the shabby exterior and figure I don't have the money to want to buy whatever it is they're selling.

I was only in the kitchen so it didn't take me long to get to the door but long enough, I saw when I looked out the spy hole, for him to start walking away. He was smartly dressed, expensive suit, not the average salesman, besides it was nearly eight o'clock, not the sort of hour for door-to-door knocking; they use the phone for that these days.

I opened the door and said "Hello?" loudly enough for him to hear, holding Tyler's collar.

He turned round and looked at the dog.

At this point, the normal thing would be for me to have said "It's alright, he's harmless" but Tyler wasn't acting right so I hung fire. I didn't recognise my visitor straight away but as he walked towards me, it didn't take long for that familiar feeling to return. Not hatred but anger. Anger that he'd taken advantage of me at my lowest.

He'd got a cut on his chin and I was looking at it as he reached the front door.

He put his hand up to the cut and rubbed it. "Shaving this morning, stupid really," he said, but I suspected a more dubious reason.

I smiled, despite it dawning on me who was standing there. "Can I help you?"

"Erm." He hesitated as Tyler gave a growl.

I just smiled again and nodded as he looked up at me.

"I'm sorry to disturb you," he continued, his charm having not lost its touch. "My car broke down just down the lane and I was wondering if I could borrow your landline – my mobile isn't picking up any signal."

"We are rather in the middle of nowhere. Sure, come in." It felt like inviting in a vampire.

Tyler gave another growl as Paul stepped forward so I picked up the dog and stepped back letting the blast from the past into my house.

He smiled as he walked and I smiled back but my smile was a different smile to his. I knew neither was genuine – we both had agendas, but at least I knew that I had the upper hand. I knew him from old and up to then, he'd not recognised me. Even when we got inside and I shut the door (I'll tell you about the door in a minute) and started speaking, he didn't twig. It took quite a while… in fact he didn't realise until I started reminding him about those years ago in a certain house in Northampstead, a pub near Wellingford, the refusal of entry, the hospital (cleverly disguised as a police cell) and so on. His face really was a picture – captured on my CCTV for posterity.

The door, yes, it's a clever piece of work. The internet is a wonderful place for information. You can do anything; build bombs, research books, change innocent-looking everyday objects into whatever you want them to be. Like a simple plastic, uPVC door, into a fortress. It had to be plastic, couldn't be wood, holds the current better. More metal in it, more locking mechanisms and so on. Clever people on the world wide web.

So, there he was at my mercy for once. With only one exit in the building and that a one-way door unless you know the trick, I could take my time. He was already late for his date, he'd told me that pretty early on in our conversation, so I was doing her a favour by keeping him here.

I let him make the call in the end but it didn't go anywhere – the outgoing line's programmed to ring itself so he gave up after getting the continuous engaged tone after a few attempts. "No hurry," he said. I think he fancied his chances. I am female.

So I poured him a drink; strongest thing in the house – he was that kind of stupid too. Maybe he thought he'd be staying over. I did give him that impression. "I'd just made dinner," I said, "and there's plenty for two".

So he jumped at the offer, probably thought it would lead to another. We were having fun; the more he drank, the more relaxed he became. I didn't need to relax and he was miles ahead of me on that score.

He seemed to tire quickly too; strange that. He looked at the clock on the wall with hazy eyes; asked if that was the right time (it was) and if he should ring the breakdown company again (he could have tried but it wouldn't have got him very far).

I reminded him what they'd said (which was nothing but he didn't twig and couldn't remember) and he soon forgot what he was waiting for.

Waiting for most people is a horrible feeling. I have nothing I need to wait for anymore but it doesn't bother me. The British are famous for our queues and I use the time to people watch; it's amazing what information you can gather without anyone opening their mouths. It's like that programme 'The Mentalist'. He can tell more about someone in the first five seconds than most people can after an evening's conversation. Patrick Jane, that was the guy.

I like making up words and ideas. I imagine the ideas fighting with each other in my brain; dip into the filing cabinet and duel with the folders containing all the other information that's in there. Some dustier than others – life part (a) and life part (b).

As I watched him fall asleep, I set my plan into action.

###

Plenty More Fish

"Plenty more fish in the sea."

You know you'll lose your temper if she says that one more time, but you nod, not looking up from the magazine you're reading, and change the subject. Tom's the reason why you're back living with your mother, and you don't want to be reminded of either. "Nancy said there might be a job going at Al Fresco."

"You're going to be a waitress?"

"Better than nothing, Mum."

"It's a start, I suppose."

You loved being a waitress while you were at university and it doesn't phase you to do it again – you've never been afraid of hard work – but...

"Of course, your father would have wanted better for you."

He would, and it does make life easier that he's no longer around, but out of the two of them, you know it's him you'd rather have standing by the kitchen sink drying the dishes you washed.

"Maybe you'll meet someone new there."

Not quite 'plenty more fish' but it grates all the same. Everything about her grates but you can't afford a B&B and don't want to impose on friends, so you pull your weight and muddle along, spending as much time with Nancy as you can.

Her name flashes up on your phone. "Hiya."

"Hi. I've spoken to Max."

You wait for her to continue. She doesn't. "Nance!"

"Sorry. I thought he was... never mind."

"And?"

"Er, yeah. He said come in at six and he'll give you a trial run."

"What?"

"Six. Trial run."

"What about an interview? Doesn't he even want to see my CV?"

"Hold on." Nancy covers the phone for a few seconds. "He says bring it, but it's only a piece of paper. Said it's all about ability and personality. Don't drop anything, impress the customers, impress him and it's yours."

"Just like that?"

"Just like that. He's not a red tape guy. Gotta go. See you at six."

"See you... and thanks."

"No problem. Will be great to see more of you."

You press the red icon, and clutch the phone.

"Good news?" the voice over your shoulder asks.

Without turning round, you reply. "Yes, I have to be there at six."

"Good," she says, and disappears upstairs.

You stick out your tongue then smile. This is the best news you've had in a while. You've never met Max but figure that if Nancy can handle him then he can't be too bad. The only Maxs you know are off the TV; the chauffeur from Hart to Hart, and Bradley's father on Eastenders. You never knew what Tanya saw in him, but then you can say that about you and Tom now. Easy to think in hindsight. A college crush gone serious then gone wrong. The teacher : student relationship that rarely works.

*

Nancy beams. "You look great!"

You look down at your plain white shirt, black skirt and comfy black shoes. You want to say "This old thing?" but you'd cut the labels off less than an hour before. "Thanks, Nance."

"OK. Come on. Let's introduce you to the great man."

You take a deep breath as you follow her through the double-swing kitchen doors. Releasing your breath comes out as a cough as Max holds out his hand. He's a little older than you, nearer Bradley's dad than the chauffeur, but much better looking and a confident, rather than sleazy, smile.

"Sorry," you say, wiping your palm on your skirt and hold out your hand.

He laughs and shakes it. "You've seen Gordon Ramsay on TV?"

You nod, slowly lowering your hand as he releases it.

"He's a pussy cat compared with me."

You go to say something about how you've always thought him not that bad, but Max continues. "Only joking. I do expect you to work hard but we play hard too. Have a laugh and a joke by all means but not out there." He points towards the restaurant's seating area. "Six to midnight, Thursday to Saturday and Monday. Tuesday lunchtimes ten 'til four. Wednesday and Sunday off. OK?"

"OK, but..."

"But?"

"You've not seen me work yet."

Max laughs. "Not here, sure, but you worked at Tantés, didn't you?"

"Yes. Yes, I did. How…" Then it dawns on you that you have seen him before, served him before. You look at Nancy and blush.

###

List of Prompts

[hot button issue you care about] has [come to pass/been squelched]. 10 years from now, what does the world look like? – Progress (409 words).

- Friday 17th May: prompt: speed – Worth every penny (147 words).
- Saturday 18th May: prompt: bubble – Bubble and squeak (169 words).
- Sunday 19th May: prompt: Jamie stood in the wreckage of his ransacked house, trying to take it all in – Wreckage (432 words).
- Monday 20th May: prompt: 16-year-old antagonist – Before Jessica (253 words).
- Tuesday 21st May: prompt: fragile protagonist – Leaving a gap (984 words).
- Wednesday 22nd May: prompt: Natalie, missing dog, gun, running water – Human Unfriendly (295 words).
- Thursday 23rd May: prompt: picture of dog and chewed cat toy – It Wasn't Me (831 words).
- Friday 24th May: prompt: a resolved noise – Scratch, squeak, bark (140 words).
- Saturday 25th May: prompt: start with the ending and work backwards – All-inclusive package (558 words).
- Sunday 26th May: prompt: official, corpulent, totem, panic, scratching, delicious – His job depended on it (100 words).
- Monday 27th May: prompt: holidays – Eight a year (145 words).
- Tuesday 28th May: prompt: children, good and bad – Billy No Mates (300 words).
- Wednesday 29th May: prompt: thwarted character – Talking when we could be walking (654 words).
- Thursday 30th May: prompt: the non-memoir – Petrified (1,250 words).
- Friday 31st May: prompt: when one door closes – Plenty more fish (724 words).

About the Author

Morgen Bailey is a writing-related blogger who spotlights authors, agents, editors and publishers. Other content includes guest posts, flash fiction, poetry, and short story and writing guide reviews.

She is also a freelance editor and offers a free 1,000-word sample edit to all new enquirers.

She runs two free monthly competitions and has been a judge for various competitions including the annual H.E. Bates Short Story Competition (first round judge 2012-2014, Head Judge 2015), NLG Flash Fiction Competition (2013-4), and RONE (2015).

The author of numerous short stories, novels, articles, she has also dabbled with poetry.

Morgen teaches creative writing across Northamptonshire (and beyond), belongs to three local writing groups, is a British Red Cross volunteer, a regular cinema visitor, and walks her dog (often while reading, writing or editing), reads (though not as often as she'd like), and in between she writes.

Everything she's involved in is detailed on her blog http://morgenbailey.wordpress.com. She can also be found chatting away about all things literary on Twitter, Facebook, LinkedIn and Tumblr.

To contact her you can also complete her website's 'Contact me' page or email her at morgen@morgenbailey.com.

Discover other titles by Morgen Bailey via https://morgenbailey.wordpress.com/books-mine.

###

Note from the Author

Thank you for purchasing this volume of the 'Story A Day May' collections, I hope you enjoyed it.

I had only learned of the existence of http://storyaday.org in April 2011 so started that project very much last minute.

As the prompts were only given each morning it was a challenge to complete a story daily with no warning, but having completed NaNoWriMo several times I enjoyed the experience, and repeated both projects in subsequent years.

I welcome feedback and always appreciate reviews of my writing.

You can find me on the links above or via email: morgen@morgenbailey.com.

Made in the USA
Charleston, SC
21 March 2016